Smudge
the Stolen
Kitten

Other titles by Holly Webb

The Snow Bear

The Reindeer Girl

The Winter Wolf

Animal Stories:

Lost in the Snow

Alfie all Alone

Lost in the Storm

Sam the Stolen Puppy

Max the Missing Puppy

Sky the Unwanted Kitten

Timmy in Trouble

Ginger the Stray Kitten

Harry the Homeless Puppy

Buttons the Runaway Puppy

Alone in the Night

Ellie the Homesick Puppy

Jess the Lonely Puppy

Misty the Abandoned Kitten

Oscar's Lonely Christmas

Lucy the Poorly Puppy

The Rescued Puppy

The Kitten Nobody Wanted

The Lost Puppy

The Frightened Kitten

The Secret Puppy

The Abandoned Puppy

The Missing Kitten

The Puppy who was Left Behind

The Kidnapped Kitten

The Scruffy Puppy

The Brave Kitten

The Forgotten Puppy

The Secret Kitten

A Home for Molly

My Naughty Little Puppy:

A Home for Rascal

New Tricks for Rascal

Playtime for Rascal

Rascal's Sleepover Fun

Rascal's Seaside Adventure

Rascal's Festive Fun

Rascal the Star

Rascal and the Wedding

Smudge the Stolen Kitten

Holly Webb

stripes

For Robin

www.hollywebbanimalstories.com

STRIPES PUBLISHING
An imprint of Little Tiger Press
1 The Coda Centre, 189 Munster Road,
London SW6 6AW

A paperback original
First published in Great Britain in 2011

Text copyright © Holly Webb, 2011
Cover illustration copyright © Sophy Williams, 2011
Inside illustrations copyright © Katherine Kirkland, 2011
Author photograph copyright © Nigel Bird
My Naughty Little Puppy illustration copyright © Kate Pankhurst

ISBN: 978-1-84715-160-5

A CIP catalogue record for this book is available
from the British Library.

Printed and bound in the UK.

10 9 8 7 6

Chapter One

There was the sound of a whistle blowing. "Ben Williams and Rob Ford! Get down from there right now!"

Olivia looked up and groaned. Mrs Mackintosh sounded as if she'd yelled right in Olivia's ear, even though she was on the other side of the playground.

"What have Ben and Rob done now?" her friend Lucie asked.

"Something awful, as usual," Olivia muttered, as they ran across the playground to see what was going on. Her big brother Ben was always in trouble at school – which wasn't fair, because all the teachers either thought that meant Olivia was naughty too, or that she ought to have stopped him. As if he'd listen to *her*! And his friend Rob was even worse.

"You're very lucky you haven't broken your necks!" the girls heard Mrs Mackintosh saying crossly. "What a stupid thing to do!"

"It isn't in the playground rules that we can't tightrope walk along the top of the fence, Mrs Mackintosh," Ben said innocently, pointing to the poster on the side of the wall.

"That's because before you, Ben, no one had even thought of it!" the head teacher snapped. "We need to add an extra rule at the bottom of that list saying that whatever idiotic thing you two think of next isn't allowed! You can miss the rest of play. Go inside and tell Mrs Beale that you're to help set out the chairs for assembly this afternoon!"

Ben winked at Olivia as he and Rob went past on their way to the hall. He didn't look as though he minded being told off at all.

Olivia sighed and Lucie gave her a sympathetic smile. "It's probably better than having a brother who's totally perfect – then everyone would ask you why you couldn't be more like him."

"I suppose," Olivia sighed, kicking at a pile of leaves. "But I can't wait till he goes to secondary school next year."

"Mrs Beale told me about what happened at lunchtime, by the way." Mum eyed Ben sternly. She worked as a part-time teaching assistant at Olivia and Ben's school.

Ben waved a forkful of spaghetti at her, looking hurt. "It's so unfair! No one had ever said we couldn't walk along the fence."

"Sometimes I think we should just send you and Rob to join the circus." Dad was trying to look cross, but Olivia could see that he was smiling.

"Excellent! No more school!" Ben grinned.

"It wasn't at all clever, Ben." Mum frowned. "I'm tempted not to tell you the special news I've got."

Olivia looked up from her pasta. "What is it? Don't be mean, Mum!"

Her mum stared up at the ceiling smiling, while Olivia and Ben begged her to tell.

"All right, all right! You remember a while ago we had a leaflet through the door about the Cat Rescue Centre?"

Olivia nodded eagerly. "With photos of all the cats they'd found new homes for! They were gorgeous. I wish we could have one. It said they were always looking for good homes for unwanted cats."

Mum smiled. "I know, Olivia – you went on about it for days. Well, Dad and I have been talking, and we decided that maybe you're both old enough to have a pet."

"Really?" Olivia gasped. "We're going to get a cat?"

"I'd rather have a dog, Mum," Ben put in. "Dogs are more fun."

Mum shook her head. "No. Dad's at work all day, and you're both at school, and so am I three days a week. A dog would get really lonely."

Ben sighed and nodded, so Mum went on quickly. "I gave the Cat Rescue Centre a ring this morning. They've got some kittens at the moment, they said, and they're ready for new homes now."

Olivia jumped up, almost upsetting her pasta into her lap. "Let's go!"

"Livvy, sit down!" Mum laughed. "The centre's not even open right now. And anyway, before we can go and choose a kitten, we have to have a home visit. To check that we're going to be suitable owners."

Olivia sat down, staring back at Mum worriedly. "Suitable? What does that mean? Do we have to know loads about cats? I only know a bit. But I've got lots of books about cats, and we could look things up on the computer…"

"Slow down!" Dad patted her shoulder. "It's OK. They're just going to want to check that our road isn't too busy. And that we're happy to put a cat flap in the kitchen door, that kind of thing."

"*And* that we don't have children who won't know how to behave around a cat," Mum said, eyeing Ben grimly. "A lady from the centre is coming to see us this evening, and we'll all have to show her that we're *sensible*, Benjamin Williams."

Ben scowled, and Olivia looked at him warily. Ben wasn't sensible at all. In fact, he was the least sensible person Olivia had ever met.

How were they ever going to convince the lady from the Rescue Centre that they were the right owners for a kitten?

"I'll give you this week's pocket money," Olivia said desperately.

Ben raised one eyebrow.

"And my Saturday sweets too! But you have to promise to be on your absolute best behaviour. Actually, don't even talk! Or – or move!"

Ben zipped his lips with his fingers,

and smirked at her, but Olivia wasn't sure she could trust him.

"Oh, there's the doorbell! Shall we go and answer it, or let Mum?" Olivia twisted her fingers together nervously. She so wanted to make a good impression.

"Mmmpfl." Ben made a strange grunting noise, and Olivia stared at him.

He shrugged. "Well, you said not to talk!"

"That doesn't mean make stupid noises! If she asks you a question you have to say something."

"Something."

"Fine, I'm keeping my pocket money." Olivia marched down the stairs feeling furious. If Ben managed to mess this up, she was never going to forgive him. Ben followed her, sniggering.

Mum was just answering the door to a friendly-looking lady in a Rescue Centre fleece.

"Hi. I'm Debbie, from the Cat Rescue Centre."

"Thanks for coming. I'm Emma and this is my husband, John, and this is Olivia and Ben." Mum led Debbie into the living room, and Olivia and Ben followed behind. Dad went to put the kettle on.

"It seems like a fairly quiet area." Debbie made a note on the sheet she was holding. "Not too many cars."

"Lots of people around here have cats," Olivia put in hopefully.

Mum laughed. "And Olivia is friends with all of them!"

Olivia perched nervously on the edge of the sofa. Ben was sitting on the sofa arm, and for once he didn't look as though he was planning anything silly. Olivia crossed her fingers. "Are there really kittens at the Rescue Centre right now?" she asked Debbie shyly.

Debbie nodded. "Two litters, actually. One's mostly ginger and white, and the other litter are a smoky grey. They're all really sweet."

Olivia's eyes shone as she imagined sitting on the sofa, just like she was now, but with a tiny grey kitten purring on her lap.

Debbie went through a long list of

questions, checking how much time the kitten would be left alone, and that Olivia's mum knew they'd have to pay for vet's bills. Olivia could see the list if she leaned over, and it mostly had ticks in the boxes. Hopefully Debbie would say yes!

Just as Debbie was handing Mum some leaflets about pet insurance and flea treatments, Dad came in with a tray of tea. He passed the cups round, then he sat down on the sofa next to Olivia. There was a sudden, very loud, very rude noise, and Dad jumped up, his face scarlet.

Ben practically fell off the sofa arm he was laughing so much, and Olivia pulled out a whoopee cushion from behind Dad.

"Ben!" Mum sounded horrified.

"I'd forgotten it was there, sorry," Ben said, but he didn't look very sorry at all.

Olivia looked over at Debbie, her eyes starting to burn with tears. Did having a stupid, rude big brother mean no kitten?

But Debbie was giggling. "I haven't seen one of those in ages. My brother used to do that all the time." Then she looked serious. "A kitten really is a big responsibility, though. And everyone in the family has to be prepared to help care for it properly." She was staring at Ben, who looked embarrassed.

"I will look after it, I promise," he muttered.

Debbie nodded. "Right then." She signed her name in swirly letters across the bottom of the form. "You can come and choose your kitten tomorrow!"

Chapter Two

Olivia doodled on her reading record book, trying to think of the best name for a beautiful little grey kitten, or perhaps a sweet gingery one. She quite liked Esmerelda, herself. But then Dad had said at breakfast that it had to be a name that they didn't mind yelling down the garden to get the kitten to come in for tea. Olivia giggled.

She couldn't really see Ben shouting, "Es–mer–el–da!"

Fluffy? Smoky? Whiskers? None of them sounded quite right. Olivia scowled down at the picture she was drawing. A kitten with big, sad eyes, just waiting for her to come and bring him home. She wished they'd been able to go to the Rescue Centre yesterday, straight after Debbie had approved them, but Mum said they needed to get everything ready first, and Olivia supposed she was right. They didn't even have a food bowl!

Lucie elbowed her in the ribs. "Mr Jones has got his eye on you, Olivia!"

Olivia straightened up and tried to look as though she was listening. She loved history usually, but today she couldn't think of anything except kittens. They were going to the pet shop after school to get everything, and then on to the Rescue Centre!

The kitten finished his bowl of biscuits and licked his paw, swiping it across his nose and ears. Then he trotted over to the wire front of the pen and stood up on his hind paws, his front claws scraping on the wire. He scrabbled at it for a moment, hoping that someone might come and open it for him. Sometimes the Rescue Centre staff came to play with the kittens, when they weren't too busy. But maybe they wouldn't, now that it was only him.

He unhooked his claws, and pattered sadly back to the cushion on the shelf in the corner. It was too big for just him – until yesterday, three small grey kittens had shared it, and now when he curled up he was lost in the middle. He missed his sisters. Even though the centre was kept warm, he still felt chilly all on his own.

"The kittens are this way." Debbie smiled at Olivia and Ben, and their mum and dad. "You haven't changed your minds then? You'd still like one?" she teased.

"Yes!" Olivia nodded so hard her bunches shook up and down. "And we've got a cat basket and a litter tray and a grooming brush and some toys and two bowls!"

Debbie laughed. "All you need is the kitten then! Come on." She led the way down the corridor, which was lined with wire-fronted enclosures. They were full of cats, all watching as Olivia walked past. She blinked, feeling suddenly sad. It wasn't that the little pens weren't nice – the cats all had a basket and toys, and most of the pens were built with a shelf, so the cats could be high up, where they felt safe. But they weren't a proper home. She wondered how often they got cuddled or stroked.

"We do take them all out every day. At least once," Debbie said quietly.

Olivia blinked. How had Debbie known what she was thinking?

"I know it doesn't look very cosy, but it's better than being out in the cold." Debbie sighed. "I'd like to take them all home, but I already have five cats... I can't really have any more..." She shook herself, and smiled firmly. "Look. The two litters of kittens are in the large pens down this side."

"Oh…" Olivia crouched down in front of the wire pen.

Four ginger kittens were bombing around, chasing each other round a scratching post and up on to a shelf where a white cat, who Olivia guessed was their mother, was trying to sleep. They scrambled over her – she looked as though she was used to it by now, her ears didn't even twitch – and then jumped down and did it all over again.

"Goodness," Mum muttered. "They're very energetic, aren't they?"

Olivia looked up at her anxiously. She hoped Mum wasn't changing her mind. "We're only going to have one," she pointed out, her voice a little squeaky with worry. "They only look bouncy because there's so many of them."

Debbie nodded. "Kittens are very energetic, but Olivia's right. Just one won't be quite so crazy. Look, we've got just one grey kitten left in the pen a little further down, he's a bit calmer."

Olivia had been so excited seeing the gorgeous ginger kittens that she'd almost forgotten there was one more.

"There were three in this litter, but two of them were rehomed yesterday. I think this little one's feeling a bit lonely." Debbie beckoned them along the corridor to the enclosure, where a small grey kitten was stretched out on his sleeping shelf, licking a paw and looking sad. He glanced up as Olivia and her family came closer, and Olivia laughed delightedly. His round green eyes gave him a permanent surprised look, and he had a dark smudge on his tail – almost as though someone had flicked a black paintbrush at him.

The kitten jumped down from his sleeping shelf, and pattered over to the wire front of the pen.

"He's so beautiful, Mum," Olivia whispered. "Look at him! He's so cute, with his little smudgy tail!"

"He is very sweet," Mum agreed.

The kitten mewed hopefully. He liked Debbie, and he knew she usually came to feed him and fuss over him. And he liked the look of the other people too. Maybe they'd pick him up. They might even take him away with them. Someone had taken his sisters, so why not him?

"Where did he come from?" Dad asked. "You don't have his mum as well, like the other kittens?"

Debbie shook her head, and sighed. "No…" She glanced at Ben and Olivia, as though she didn't want to upset them. "These kittens were abandoned. A lady out for a walk by the canal found them. Someone had just left them in a cardboard box."

Olivia stared at the kitten, who was pawing hopefully at the wire. How could someone just have abandoned him?

"They were lucky to be found so quickly," Debbie added. "They were only two weeks old; they would have died if they'd been left much longer without food." She patted Olivia's arm, seeing how upset she was. "But the good thing about it is that the kittens were bottle-fed, which means they're super-friendly. This one is a little love. He wants to be cuddled all the time."

"Can we have him?" Olivia turned round. "Ben, don't you think he's gorgeous?"

"I suppose. The ginger ones were really fun, but he looks friendly, too," Ben said.

"Let's get him out so you can give him a stroke," Debbie suggested.

"Oh, yes please…" Olivia gazed through the wire at the kitten. He was scrabbling at it now, looking as though he liked the idea too. Debbie opened the front of the pen, and laughed as he scampered out before she could catch him.

The kitten skidded to a stop in front of Olivia's feet, and glanced up, suddenly shy. He looked at Olivia sideways, obviously wondering who she was and if she was friendly.

Olivia stretched out her fingers to him, and he sniffed them, and then rubbed the side of his face up and down her hand. "Ahhh. Do you think I could pick him up?" she asked Debbie.

"Give it a try. Don't worry if he wriggles away, he'll probably be a bit excited."

But the kitten snuggled happily against Olivia's school jumper, and purred. This was just what he wanted. So much better than being all alone in the pen, and the girl smelled nice.

Olivia stroked him gently behind the ears. His fur was soft and velvety, and he nuzzled a tiny, cold pink nose into her neck, making her giggle. "Oh, listen to him purring! He feels like a little lawn mower!"

The kitten closed his eyes happily, and kneaded his paws into Olivia's shoulder.

Debbie smiled. "He's definitely taken to you."

Olivia's eyes glowed as she looked up at her parents, kitten paws tangled in her jumper. "Please can we have him?"

"But what about the ginger ones?" Ben grumbled, but then he stroked the top of the kitten's head. "I guess he is quite cute," he admitted.

Dad nodded, smiling. "So what are we going to call him then?"

In the end, the name was obvious. Smudge just fitted. Olivia's mum suggested Alfie, and Ben wanted to call him after his favourite footballer, but Smudge just looked like Smudge.

He fitted into the house too. Debbie had said that he was already house-trained. She'd also explained that Smudge had had all his vaccinations, and was safe to go outside, but it would be better not to let him out on his own for the first couple of weeks, while he got used to his new home. Dad was glad about that, as it gave him a bit longer to fit the cat flap.

On his first night, Olivia had left Smudge curled up in his new basket.

She'd lined up all his toys next to him, and given him one of her old toy cats in case he was lonely. Then she'd refilled his water bowl, and given him a prawn-flavour cat treat as a bedtime snack.

"Olivia, it's way past your bedtime!" Mum put an arm round her shoulders. "He'll be fine. He's used to the Rescue Centre. I'm sure our kitchen's much nicer than that pen he was in."

Olivia nodded. "Yes, but he doesn't know our house yet, and he doesn't understand what's happening. What if he thinks we're never coming back?"

"Come on. You're not sleeping in the kitchen with him, Livvy."

Olivia sighed and looked back sadly as Mum shooed her out. The light from the hallway gleamed in the kitten's huge eyes. He looked sad too.

Upstairs, Olivia got ready for bed. But she couldn't stop thinking about Smudge, alone in the dark kitchen. Perhaps she should just go and check on him?

Ben was lying on his bed reading, and he glanced up as Olivia went past. "Mum'll hear if you sneak downstairs, Olivia. She always catches me."

Olivia leaned round his bedroom door. "How did you know what I was doing?" she hissed. "I might just have been going to the loo!"

Ben shrugged. "I could tell by the way you were looking at the stairs." He frowned. "Hey, is that Smudge making that noise?"

From downstairs came a faint but pitiful wailing, along with a scratching sound. The noise of kitten claws scrabbling at a kitchen door.

Olivia hung over the banisters, listening to the sad little howls.

Eventually Mum came out of the living room, frowning. "I hope he's all right," she said over her shoulder to Dad. "Oh, Olivia. Is he keeping you awake?"

"Can't we let him come upstairs?" Olivia pleaded. "He sounds so lonely."

Mum sighed and glanced at Dad.

Dad shrugged. "Well, he is house-trained."

"Thank you!" Olivia smiled with delight, and ran down the stairs to open the kitchen door.

Smudge shot out, and she gathered him into her arms, cuddling him against her pyjamas. "Don't worry, Smudge," she whispered. "I'll look after you." She carried him upstairs, and put him down gently on her bed.

Smudge looked around interestedly, and padded up and down Olivia's duvet, inspecting it carefully. Olivia tried not to laugh. He looked so serious. Then he marched over to her pillow, curled himself up in the hollow between the pillow and the duvet, and went to sleep.

Chapter Three

Smudge had only been there a few days, but Olivia's house was definitely his home now. He had explored every possible hole and hiding place, and got stuck in several of them. But Olivia or Ben or their parents were always there to rescue him. Except for today. Dad was at work, Olivia and Ben had gone to school that morning, and as it was

Thursday their mum had to go into school to work too. Smudge was all on his own for the first time, and he didn't like it. He wandered around the house, his tail twitching. He'd already been into every room that was open, and he knew that no one was there, but he kept hoping that maybe if he looked again he would find somebody.

He padded back into the kitchen, and sniffed hopefully at the door. Olivia and Ben had taken him out into the garden when they got home from school yesterday. It had been his first taste of the outside world, and his ears flickered back and forth as he remembered watching the birds, and chasing after the little jingly ball that Olivia had rolled along the patio.

There it was, in the corner by the kitchen cupboards. Smudge trotted over and patted the ball with one paw. It rolled along, the little bell jingling, and he pounced on it. The ball slid along the polished tiles, and so did Smudge, rolling over on to his back, wriggling and clawing at it. But then the ball slid away from his paws and stopped against the kitchen table leg, and it wasn't as much fun any more.

Grumpily, Smudge lay there on his back, licking his paws. He'd already had quite a long sleep in the recycling box on the kitchen counter. (Ben had emptied it that morning, and it was just the right size for Smudge to feel cosy in, much better than his basket.) Now he wanted someone to play with.

Perhaps by the time he got upstairs, Olivia would be back in her bedroom? He trotted through to the hallway and started to struggle up the stairs. He was big enough to climb them, but it was an effort, and he had to scrabble and heave himself up each step. He sat down for a little while at the top of the stairs, his sides heaving, and then he crept along the landing and nosed his way round Olivia's door.

She wasn't there. The room was empty.

Smudge crept under Olivia's bed. He picked his way between two tottering piles of books, and pounced on the flex of Olivia's hair-dryer. Then, yawning, he snuggled himself inside her gym bag. He liked small spaces, and climbing the stairs had worn him out. When he woke up, surely they would all be back?

"I can't believe it's only lunchtime," Olivia muttered, checking her watch for the hundredth time.

"Are you missing Smudge?" Lucie grinned at her.

Olivia nodded. "It's the first time we've left him alone all day. I really hope he's OK. He nearly climbed out of the living-room window yesterday. I caught him just as he was sticking his head out."

"He still isn't allowed out then? Isn't he old enough?"

"He's ten weeks, so he could go outside, but Debbie said it's best if we wait until we've had him a bit longer before letting him out on his own. It already feels like he's been with us for ages, though. He isn't shy or nervous at all." Then she shook her head. "Except for yesterday, when we took Smudge into the garden with us, and Ben got him with his water pistol. He *said* it was an accident, but I don't know…"

Lucie sighed. "I'm so jealous. I love Tiger, but he's really old and just sleeps all day. Can I come and see Smudge soon?" she asked hopefully.

Olivia nodded. She was desperate to show off how gorgeous Smudge was. "Do you want to come to tea tomorrow? Mum's doing playground duty, we could go and ask her."

They ran over to Olivia's mum, who was turning the end of a skipping rope for a bunch of year one girls. "Mum, can Lucie come to tea tomorrow? She really wants to see Smudge."

Mum frowned. "Oh, not Friday, Lucie, sorry. Ben's already invited Rob. I'll ask your mum about popping over at the weekend," she suggested, and Lucie nodded, looking pleased, but Olivia was frowning.

"Rob's coming? To tea? Mum, does

he have to? Ben always plays up when Rob's round, they'll be awful! They might upset Smudge!"

"I'm sure they won't, Olivia. Oh dear! Up you get, Sinead!" One of the year ones had tripped over the rope, and Mum went to pick her up.

Olivia sighed, and glanced at Lucie. "I bet they will. You know what Ben's like. And with Rob there he's three times as bad. I'll just have to keep Smudge with me the whole time."

"Smudge! Where are you, puss?" As soon as Olivia got home from school, she dropped her bag, pulled off her coat, and dashed upstairs to search for him.

Maybe he was having a sleep on her bed? As she pushed her bedroom door wide open, there was a little mew and Smudge wriggled out from under her bed. A pile of books toppled over as he shot out and scrambled into her lap. Olivia giggled. "Mum's right, I really do need to tidy up, especially if you're going to go exploring under there. Those books nearly squashed your tail!" She settled down to do her homework with Smudge purring on her knee. When she'd finished she carried him downstairs, and wandered into the kitchen to talk to Mum. Ben was out in the garden building a den in the apple tree.

"Mum, does Rob have to come to tea tomorrow?"

Mum looked up from the saucepan she was stirring. "Well, yes. It's all arranged. What's the matter, Livvy?"

Olivia shrugged. "I don't want him to…" she whispered. "He does stupid stuff, and he makes Ben do stupid stuff too. They always get into trouble."

Mum sighed. "I know they're a bit naughty. But Rob is Ben's best friend. Can't you just stay out of their way tomorrow, love?"

"But what if they upset Smudge? Can I take him up to my room tomorrow to keep him out of their way too?"

Mum looked at her seriously for a moment, and shook her head. "Olivia, Ben wants to show Smudge off to Rob. I know you really love Smudge, and he's taken to you so well, but he's not just yours, sweetheart. He's Ben's kitten as well."

Olivia nodded miserably. She knew Mum was right, but it didn't help. Smudge *felt* like he was her kitten, and she didn't want the boys anywhere near him.

"Hello, Smudge!" Olivia's dad walked in, and tickled the kitten under the chin.

Then Ben flung open the kitchen door, and stomped muddy footprints across the floor. "Is it dinnertime yet?"

"Shoes off!" Mum grabbed him. "And then it is, yes."

Olivia rolled her eyes at Mum. "You see?" she muttered. She let Smudge down to the floor and went to help pass the bowls of pasta round.

"What?" Ben asked, as he hopped around taking off his trainers.

Olivia folded her arms. "I just don't think it's a good idea for you to have Rob over tomorrow. Not when we've only had Smudge for three days. Rob'll probably get Smudge to ... to climb trees or something. You always do stupid things with him! Like that time you dug a tunnel and pulled up all Dad's daffodil bulbs!"

Ben shook his head. "That *so* isn't fair! For a start, we didn't know they were there! And anyway, Rob loves cats. He's been asking his mum and dad for one for ages. He can't wait to meet Smudge."

"Oh…" Olivia muttered.

"Actually, where is Smudge?" Mum asked.

Olivia looked down, expecting to see him by her feet, hoping to be fed. But he wasn't there.

"I don't know." Olivia went to look in the hallway, but then there was a worried little meow from somewhere on the other side of the kitchen.

Mum frowned. "Where on earth is he?"

The meowing got louder.

"I think he's behind the cooker!" Ben said suddenly.

"But it's still hot from cooking dinner!" Mum cried.

Olivia dashed over to the cooker. "Smudge, come out of there!"

But Smudge only mewed louder.

"He's stuck," Olivia muttered, crouching down and trying to reach behind the cooker. "Ow, and it's hot. I can't get to him. I think he got trapped and now he can't turn round!"

Dad shook his head. "What is it with that kitten? The smaller the space, the more he likes it. I'll have to pull it out a bit."

He dragged the cooker out from the wall, and Smudge darted out and ran to Olivia. He was trembling, and covered in dust balls – he looked even furrier than usual.

Mum shook her head. "I don't think Smudge needs the boys to get him into trouble, Olivia. He can manage it perfectly well on his own!"

Chapter Four

After school on Friday, Olivia ran into the house ahead of Rob and Ben, looking for Smudge.

The little grey kitten slipped round the living-room door, mewing excitedly, and purred as she picked him up. Olivia stroked him lovingly, and then took a step back as Rob came over to her. She was used to Rob racing around the playground with Ben, chasing people and getting into trouble. She wasn't sure he knew how to be careful with a kitten.

"Hey! He's really cute!"

Olivia nodded slowly.

"Can I stroke him? Will he mind?" Even Rob's voice was gentler than usual.

"Um, OK…" Olivia looked on anxiously, but Rob tickled Smudge behind the ears – his favourite place, and Smudge purred and wriggled so that Olivia had to hand him over, letting him fasten his claws in Rob's school sweater.

"He likes you!" Ben commented. "Come on, bring him up to my room." He grabbed Smudge's favourite jingly ball and a squeaky mouse.

"But…" Olivia watched as the boys thundered up the stairs, taking Smudge with them. She started to run after them, but Mum called her back. "Leave them on their own, Olivia."

"But they've taken Smudge up there. What are they going to do with him?"

Mum laughed. "Just play with him, like you do! Rob seems to really like him. Come on, Livvy. Come and make some chocolate-chip cookies with me, we can have them after tea."

Olivia sighed. She supposed Mum was right. Maybe she was just feeling jealous because Smudge seemed to like Rob.

They were in the middle of cutting out the biscuits, when Ben and Rob and Smudge came down to watch TV.

Olivia looked at Smudge carefully, but he seemed to be all right. The boys hadn't trimmed his whiskers, or painted him blue, or done any of the other stupid things she'd been imagining.

A little later, Ben came into the kitchen. "Are the cookies ready yet? They smell fantastic."

"The first trayful are nearly done, but they're for after tea, Ben! We're having fish fingers. And I can see you stealing the chocolate!" Mum waved a spoon at him, as Ben popped a handful of choc drops into his mouth, grinning.

"Where's Smudge?" Olivia asked anxiously.

"Sitting on the sofa with Rob – calm down, Olivia! He's fine. Rob thinks he's great."

Olivia stared out of the kitchen door, hoping Smudge might come in to see her. But he stayed with Rob.

Smudge yawned, and stretched out his paws. Rob was stroking him very nicely, but he wanted to go and see what Olivia was doing. He hadn't seen her all day, and he wanted her to play with him. And he was hungry. There were food smells coming from the kitchen, good fishy smells, he thought. He stood up sleepily, getting ready to jump off Rob's lap.

Rob looked down. "Where are you going, Smudge?" He tickled him under the chin and Smudge purred. Maybe he wouldn't go just yet.

"Ben's so lucky," Rob murmured gently. "I wish I had a kitten like you." He sighed, and picked up his school bag from the floor, rooting around in it.

Smudge peered over, and stuck his nose in. It smelled good.

Rob laughed. "I'm just looking for my Polos, but I don't think they're good for cats. Oh, I bet I know what you can smell. My leftover ham sandwich." He laughed again as Smudge stuck his whole head in the bag. "Where are you going?"

Smudge could smell the delicious ham at the bottom of the bag, and he wriggled all the way in.

"Hey, Ben's going to think I'm taking you home." Rob grinned. But then his smile faded a little. Smudge popped his head out of the bag, licking round his jaws hopefully. "There isn't any more, Smudge, sorry."

The little kitten yawned widely, and ducked back into the bag, curling up at the bottom and closing his eyes.

Rob shook his head. "I can't believe you're asleep in my school bag." He stared at Smudge thoughtfully and sighed. "I really could take you home…"

"Mrs Williams…"

"Oh, hello, Rob. Do you want to help with the cookies?"

Rob was standing by the kitchen door, looking shifty. "Um. No. I have to go home. Um, I feel sick."

"Oh dear!" Olivia's mum put down the tray of biscuits, and hurried over to him.

Ben and Olivia stared at Rob in surprise. "You don't look ill," Ben said.

"Has it just suddenly come over you?" Olivia's mum asked. "Are you hot?"

Rob backed away from her, and nodded. "Yes. And I feel *really* sick. Please can I ring my mum?"

"Of course." She handed him the phone. "You poor thing."

Rob took the phone out into the hallway, and they could hear him explaining urgently to his mum.

"He does sound very upset, poor Rob," Olivia's mum said anxiously.

"He was fine ten minutes ago," Ben muttered.

Olivia frowned. "I bet he's broken something. And he doesn't want to get into trouble. Did he mess anything up in your room?"

"Don't be silly, Olivia. The boys have just been watching TV. How could he have broken anything?" Mum glared at her crossly. "You mustn't be mean."

"She's coming." Rob stood at the

kitchen door, holding out the phone to Olivia's mum.

Rob's mum arrived a few minutes later, and Olivia's mum chatted to her, while Rob lurked impatiently by the door. "I'm really sorry. I don't think it's anything he's eaten – we hadn't even had tea."

Rob's mum shook her head. "It's probably just something going round – I only hope he hasn't given it to Ben and Olivia. At least he's got the weekend to recover. Anyway, I'd better get him home. Thank you for having him!"

Rob darted into the living room and came out carrying his school bag. He was holding it against his tummy, hunching over, and his mum looked at him worriedly. "Oh dear, you do look as though you might be sick. Come on, let's get you home." She led him down the path to the car.

Mum closed the door and hurried into the kitchen. "I'd forgotten about the fish fingers with all of that going on; I'm afraid they might be a bit crispy…"

"Can Smudge have one of Rob's ones?" Olivia asked. "I bet he'd love a fish finger." Then she jumped up suddenly. "Where is Smudge?" she asked, her voice a little panicky. "I haven't seen him in ages. Rob was cuddling him in the living room."

"Perhaps Rob shut the living-room door?" Mum suggested, as she served up tea. "He's probably stuck in there."

But the living-room door was open and there was no Smudge on the sofa, or hiding behind it to leap out at Olivia as she searched around. She darted upstairs to look in her room.

"Smudge! Smudge! Mum, he's not in there, and I've checked upstairs, and I can't find him anywhere!" Olivia ran back into the kitchen.

Ben was sitting at the table eating a huge pile of fish fingers – his and Rob's. "He'll be under your bed or something. I'll come and help you look." But Smudge wasn't in either of their rooms, and he hadn't climbed into the bath and got stuck. He wasn't in the airing cupboard on the towels either.

"Could he have got out somehow?" Ben asked when they came back downstairs.

Mum frowned. "I'm sure all the windows were shut. After he nearly got out yesterday I was a bit worried he might try that again."

Olivia nodded. "I checked all the windows this morning, before we went to school."

Mum sighed. "Smudge must be hiding somewhere, like he always does. He'll pop out at us in a minute, I'm sure."

Olivia turned to Ben, her hands on her hips. "Did you and Rob let him outside?"

Ben stared at her, wide-eyed. "He was just watching TV with us, Olivia. We didn't even *go* out, so how's it our fault suddenly?"

"I bet that's why Rob wanted to go home." Olivia sat down on a chair as her knees suddenly felt shaky. "He was scared he was going to get into trouble. You let him out. I can't believe you'd do that!" she yelled.

"Olivia!" Mum warned. "You're just jumping to conclusions."

"We didn't let him out!" Ben stood up angrily. "How many times do I have to say it?" He stomped out of the kitchen, muttering. "I'm going to look for him upstairs. He must be here somewhere."

Olivia slumped on her chair, feeling tears welling up in her eyes. However much Ben denied it, she was sure the boys had let Smudge get out – either by accident, or as part of some stupid game. Smudge was so little! He'd only been outside once, and he'd had her and Ben there to make sure he didn't escape from the garden, or get himself stuck somewhere. Just thinking of all the places where he might hurt himself made her feel sick.

Chapter Five

Smudge woke up, and was surprised to find that everything was dark, and the bag was bumping around. The little kitten swayed from side to side, mewing with fright. Where was Olivia? Why was he stuck in here? He needed Olivia to let him out!

"Hey, ssshhh. I'm going to get you out of there."

The bag opened, and Smudge could see Rob peering inside. He gave a soft little mew. This wasn't right. He had thought that Olivia would come and find him. He cowered back against the bottom of the bag, and hissed as Rob tried to open it up a bit more. The boy had been kind before, stroking and cuddling him, and feeding him sandwiches, but now Smudge was confused, and he wanted Olivia.

"Hey, Smudge. Don't you want to get out? Come and see my bedroom," Rob said, gently reaching in to pick up the kitten.

Smudge spat crossly as a warning, and when Rob didn't take his hand away, he clawed at it, hard.

"Ow!" Rob sat back, sucking at the bleeding scratch. Then he sighed. "OK. I suppose I'd scratch if I got shut up in a bag and bounced around all over the place. Maybe I'd better get you something else to eat." He smiled at Smudge. "You liked that ham sandwich, didn't you?"

Smudge saw him stand up.

"I'll go and see what's in the fridge, but I might be a while. Mum still thinks I'm sick, so I'll have to wait till she's not looking. Back soon. Here, you can play with this ball, it's got spikes, look! That'd be fun, wouldn't it? See you in a minute, Smudge."

The bedroom door clicked, and Smudge waited, his heart thumping. Had the boy gone? Was it safe to come out?

Slowly, cautiously, he wriggled out of the bag.

"I can't find him anywhere." Ben was standing in the doorway, and his voice had changed. He wasn't angry any more, he sounded frightened.

"I told you so!" Olivia swiped a hand across her eyes. "You must have opened a window, or let him out of the kitchen door, or something!"

"We didn't! You and Mum were in the kitchen the whole time, how could we let him out of here?"

"Ben's right, Olivia, you're not being fair."

"Even if Ben didn't let him out, his stupid friend did!" Olivia sobbed. "And now Smudge is lost!"

"I didn't let him out, I promise I didn't, and Rob didn't either. He would have said if something had happened." Ben's voice was shaking now.

"Both of you calm down. Olivia, try

and stop crying, sweetheart, it's only making you feel worse. Come on. We'll all do another proper search round the house. Look at yesterday, when Smudge got himself stuck behind the oven! He's around somewhere, I'm sure of it."

Olivia shook her head. "Then why can't we hear him? If he was here and stuck, he'd be meowing, Mum. Wouldn't he?"

Mum got up. "Maybe you're right. If Smudge was shut in somewhere, we'd hear him. We'd better go and check outside. Maybe there's a window open that we've missed."

"I told you!" Olivia wailed. "Rob let him out, he must have done."

Even Ben was looking less certain now. "Rob wouldn't just let him out –

I told him Smudge wasn't allowed outside on his own yet..."

They hurried out into the garden, calling and calling, but apart from next-door's cat, Lily, who looked very curiously at them, the garden was empty. It was starting to get dark, and cold. Olivia shivered, thinking of Smudge outside in the chilly wind.

"What about the garden shed?" Mum suggested, trying to think of places a kitten might find interesting. "Could he have squeezed himself in there somehow?"

The shed door was tightly shut, but they checked anyway. And under the patio furniture, and behind the pile of flower pots, and even up the cherry tree.

Smudge was nowhere to be found.

"You two stay here, I'll just go and ask Sally next door if she's seen him," Mum said. "Why don't you go and have another look inside?"

"I'm sorry I said you let him out," Olivia muttered, as they peered behind the sofa. "I know you wouldn't really."

"Do you think he'll be all right?"

Ben asked miserably. "I just don't see where he can be!"

Olivia stood up again, and went to check behind the curtains, but then she stopped. "Rob forgot his lunchbox," she said slowly, pointing at a Star Wars lunchbox down by the side of the sofa. "And a load of his books, look. His reading record and everything…"

Ben frowned. "Why would he take all that stuff out of his bag?"

"His bag... He was carrying it in a funny way." Olivia stared at Ben, her eyes wide. "Ben, he didn't let Smudge out, he *stole* him! Rob put Smudge in his school bag and took him home!"

"Don't be stupid," Ben said, but he was chewing his thumbnail worriedly. "He wouldn't... What's he going to do, hide Smudge in his room? I know he really wanted a pet, but he wouldn't steal our cat..."

"I bet you he did," Olivia told him grimly. She heard the sound of the key in the lock, and rushed out into the hallway. "Mum! We think we know where Smudge is!"

Chapter Six

Smudge gazed around the room. He had no idea where he was, but he knew this wasn't home and he wanted to get away. His ears were laid back, listening for footsteps. But no one was coming. He had to get out and find Olivia. He shook his head, feeling dazed from bumping around in the bag. His nose was still full of the smell of ham sandwich, and the musty scent of the inside of the bag, but there was something else...

The window was open! Smudge's eyes widened a little.

Rob's bed was pushed up against the wall. If he could jump on to that, it was only a little climb to the windowsill. But the bed was very high up. Much higher than the steps on the stairs he'd struggled with. Smudge glanced anxiously round at the door. He was sure the boy would be back soon. He had to be quick. With a huge effort, he ran at the bed, hooking his claws into the duvet cover and scrabbling upwards furiously. From the top of the bed it didn't look such a small climb to the windowsill after all, but Rob had nice

long curtains. Smudge raced up them,
his heart hammering, leaving a pattern
of little hooked loops all the way up.
And then he scrambled up on to the
windowsill.

He peered out of the open window, his nose twitching, trying to see where to go next. But below him was only a straight wall down to the garden. Smudge teetered on the edge of the window, his tail flicking anxiously back and forth. He had to get out, and this was the only way. He edged a little further, on to the outside windowsill. He could see all the way along the garden, and he was sure that if he could get down there, he could find his way back to Olivia somehow. But it was a long way to jump… He paced up and down, mewing pitifully. He was cold, out there on the windowsill. The sky was darkening, and there was a chill wind ruffling his fur. It shook the branches of the tree in the corner of the garden, and they kept tapping against the wall and scraping the windowsill.

Smudge crouched on the windowsill, shivering, and watching the twigs brushing against the wall. It was the only way down, but the branches were like thin little fingers. He had never climbed a tree, and certainly never climbed *down* one.

Suddenly, Smudge whipped round. He could hear the door handle turning. He had to go now! He sprang on to the nearest branch that looked strong enough to hold him, and mewed with fright as it wobbled and dipped underneath him. He clung on desperately, digging his claws into the bark, and wailed as a gust of wind shook the tree again.

He scrabbled his way along the branch towards the tree trunk, and skidded and bumped down to the fence, where he perched, mewing with fright. It was a very narrow fence, but at least it wasn't shaking – or not as much as the tree had been.

Smudge teetered, trying to work out which way to jump. Back into the garden? But then the boy might come and find him. So, down the other side of the fence? There was long grass down there that looked soft enough to jump on to. But he had no idea where the alley went, or if it would lead back to Olivia. There were only a few battered-looking garages.

He jumped, bouncing down the side of the fence, and landing in a flurry of paws on the soft grass. Now where should he go?

"Yes, Rob's here, I'll just get him, Ben."

Ben put his hand over the phone

receiver and nodded to Olivia and Mum. "He's coming."

Olivia sat forward on the sofa, trying to listen, and Ben rolled his eyes and pressed the speakerphone button. Rob's voice echoed out into the room.

"What is it?" He sounded jumpy and worried.

"Where's Smudge?" Ben demanded.

"What do you mean?"

"He knows!" Olivia hissed. Rob was trying to sound as though he didn't understand, but he wasn't very good at it.

"We found all your stuff. You took him away in your school bag, didn't you?" Ben said angrily.

"I'm sorry..." Rob muttered finally. "It was all a mistake. Smudge was sniffing around my bag, and then he

88

climbed in and went to sleep. I just wanted to have him for a bit to see what it would be like…"

"You stole him!" Olivia yelled down the phone. "Bring him back now!"

There was silence. Then Rob whispered, "I can't…"

"What do you mean, you can't?" Ben asked.

"He's gone." Rob sounded almost like he was crying.

"You've *lost* him!" Olivia cried.

"I think he got out of my bedroom window," Rob gulped. "He must have done. I searched my whole room, and he just wasn't anywhere. I'm sorry."

Mum reached out for the phone. "Rob, can you get your mother for me, please."

Olivia didn't even hear as her mum and Rob's tried to sort out what was going on. She was slumped on the sofa, her hands squashed into her eyes to stop herself from crying.

Eventually Mum ended the call, and put one arm round Olivia, and one round Ben.

"It looks like Rob did take Smudge," she said slowly. "His mum said she couldn't believe he'd do something so stupid. He hadn't told her what had happened. She's really sorry."

"What are we going to do?" Olivia wailed. "Can we go round to Rob's house and look for Smudge?"

"Rob's dad just came home, and he's going out to look, and ask all the neighbours," Mum explained. "I don't think there's much point in us going over there, it's almost dark. Rob's mum said he thinks Smudge must have been gone for about half an hour, he could have got away down the road."

"But it's so cold," Olivia whispered. "Smudge is out there all on his own!"

Chapter Seven

Smudge was still hiding in the long grass, wondering what to do. He was dreadfully hungry. If he was at home, he was sure it would be teatime. A bowl of crunchy biscuits, or perhaps some of the meaty stuff he really liked. The thought of food made him more determined. He had to go home. He crept out of the clump of grass, and looked around the alleyway worriedly. He had no idea if he was close to Olivia's house or not.

Perhaps he could call for Olivia? But then, he was still very close to the house. What if that boy heard him?

He took a few steps down the alley, his fur prickling. The air felt strange, and it was making him edgy. He carried on, hoping desperately that he would see some sign of Olivia. Wouldn't she come and look for him? Now he was further away from Rob's house, he risked mewing hopefully. But no one was around to hear him.

A large raindrop landed suddenly on his nose, and he jumped back in surprise. It was followed by another and another, and in seconds Smudge's fur was soaked and clinging to him. The rain was followed by a strange eerie flash that seemed to split the dark sky and then a rolling boom of thunder. Smudge shot across the alley to the tumbledown garages, looking for a place to hide. They were all locked up, but he spotted a hole, where a brick had come loose, and squeezed himself inside. There was another crash of thunder. Startled, he jumped back, bumping into a pile of boxes and paint tins, which fell clattering all around him.

Smudge scampered away with a terrified squeak. When he looked back, he saw that a heavy wooden box had fallen right in front of his hole. He was trapped.

He sprang forward, frantically mewing and clawing at the box, but it was far too heavy for him to move.

At last he stopped scrabbling, and sat back, exhausted. He wove his way through the dusty darkness, round the piles of boxes and bikes and all sorts of rubbish that was stored in the garage, hoping to find another hole. But he couldn't find even the tiniest gap.

Miserably he settled down on a pile of old dust sheets. It was cold, and he was starving, and he wanted to be on Olivia's lap on the sofa. Sadly, he snuffled himself to sleep.

"Look at the rain," Olivia whispered, peering out of the living-room window.

Mum came up behind her, and hugged her. "I'm sure he's tucked himself away somewhere safe. We'll find him tomorrow."

"He's only ever been out in the garden with us." Olivia turned to look at Mum, her eyes wide and worried. "He's never been out in the rain! And the thunder's so scary, he must be terrified."

"Like you," Ben muttered from her doorway. But he didn't seem to be putting much effort into teasing her. He sounded too miserable to bother. He came over to the window, and stared at the rain. "Rob's dad phoned just now. He's asked all the neighbours to look out for Smudge, but he had to stop looking and come back inside – he said he couldn't see anything, it was raining so hard."

Their dad came in, carrying the phone. "Olivia, it's Lucie on the phone for you."

Olivia took the phone reluctantly. She wasn't sure whether she wanted to talk to Lucie or not. She desperately wanted to tell someone how angry she was with Rob, but at the same time she didn't want to have to say that Smudge was missing.

"Hi, Olivia! Mum says I can come round to yours tomorrow, if you like. Would that be OK with your mum?"

"I don't know…" Olivia whispered, her eyes prickling with tears.

"Oh, are you going out?" Lucie's voice was disappointed. "I was hoping we could play with Smudge. I really want to see him!"

Olivia sniffed, and then sobbed. "He's gone!"

There was a confused silence on the other end of the line. "You mean, he had to go back to the Rescue Centre?" Lucie said at last.

"No. You know Rob was coming for tea with Ben – he took him."

"Rob Ford stole your kitten?" Lucie sounded as though she didn't quite believe it.

Olivia gave a cross little laugh. "I know it sounds stupid, but he really did! He even owned up to it. But then Smudge tried to get away from him and climbed out of his bedroom window, and now we don't know where he is!"

"What are you going to do?" Lucie whispered in horror.

"We're going to look for him tomorrow – Mum says it's too dark to go round there now. But he could be anywhere, Lucie. And it's a horrible night."

"Can I come and help you look? I bet my mum will come too. The more people the more chance there is we'll spot him," Lucie suggested.

For the first time since she'd realized Smudge was gone, Olivia felt a little bit better. "Would you really help look?"

"Call me tomorrow and let me know when," Lucie told her firmly. "We'll find him."

"OK," Olivia whispered. "Thanks, Lucie. See you in the morning." She put the phone back in its cradle. "Lucie's going to come over and help us look," she explained to Mum and Dad.

Dad nodded. "That's nice of her. Look, I think you should go to bed. You're only sitting here making yourself feel worse. And we want to get up early and go and look for Smudge."

Olivia nodded, and went up to her room, but she didn't think she'd be able to get to sleep. And when she did, she was sure she was going to dream about Smudge all night. Smudge lost and all alone, and wondering why she hadn't come to find him.

She lay in her warm bed, listening to the rain drumming on the roof outside her window, and hoping that Smudge was tucked away somewhere safe. But he could be anywhere, she thought worriedly, turning over, and huddling under her duvet. What if they never found him? What would they say to the people from the Rescue Centre? Debbie had said they would call in the next few days to see how they were getting on, and whether Smudge was settling in. They would have to tell her that they had lost him! Or actually, that a stupid, selfish, idiot boy had stolen him.

Olivia thumped her pillow. At least being angry with Rob had stopped her wanting to cry. She wondered if someone could be sent to prison for stealing a kitten. Rob certainly deserved it. Dreamily, she imagined Rob in handcuffs, and herself standing there, with Smudge purring in her arms, watching as the police led him away.

It seemed so real. For a moment, she could hear Smudge purring, she was sure. But it was only the rain, beating against her window.

Chapter Eight

Smudge woke up, shivering. Although he had huddled himself into the pile of dustsheets, it was freezing inside the garage. He felt so cold he could hardly move. At last he stood up gingerly, stretching out his paws and fluffing up his fur to keep himself as warm as possible. He was sure that he was colder because he was so hungry. The last food he'd had was the sandwich in that boy's bag yesterday afternoon, and now he felt horribly empty.

It was getting light. There were dirty, greyish windows at the top of the walls, just under the roof, and a little watery sunshine was fighting its way in. Somehow it made Smudge feel more cheerful, even if it wasn't making him much warmer. In the light he could see that the garage was full of piles of old junk – bits of cars and bikes, piles of pots of paint, and lots of dust. Last night it had just been strange shapes that wobbled when he scurried past them. It was all a lot less scary in the daylight.

He jumped down from his pile of dust sheets, his legs still stiff and achy from the cold, and started to search for a way out. Last night, with the rain pouring down, the garage had at least been a shelter. Now it was stopping him going home to Olivia, and he was determined to escape. Surely now it was lighter he would be able to find another hole somewhere? Smudge made his way along the wall, sniffing and nudging at the concrete blocks.

Edging round the side of a large box, his whiskers twitched hopefully as he spotted a little light coming through a crack at the bottom of the wall. He nosed at it eagerly, and then his whiskers drooped again. It was such a very small gap. But he had to try. The rest of the walls were made from solid concrete blocks, but here one of the blocks seemed to have broken, and it had been patched up with a metal sheet on the outside. If he wriggled into the dark gap between the blocks, there was a tiny hole. Perhaps if he clawed at it for a while, it might give way?

Smudge scrabbled hopefully, his tiny claws making an eerie screeching noise against the rough metal sheet. He scratched and scraped for what seemed like ages, till his claws ached, but when he stopped and pressed his nose against the hole, it didn't seem to have got any bigger at all...

"Olivia! What time is it?" Dad moaned.

"Um, half-past five. You said we'd get up early and go straight round to Rob's!"

"I meant more like seven..." Dad murmured wearily.

"Go back to bed until half-past six,"

Mum added. "We can't go and wake up Rob's family this early."

Olivia sighed. She supposed Mum was right. But she had been lying awake since five, watching her bedroom get lighter and lighter. As soon as it seemed to be light enough to search for a kitten, she had got up.

She mooched back into her room, and lay down on her bed. She wasn't going to be able to go back to sleep. Instead she grabbed a notebook from her bedside table, and started to make a list of things it would be useful to take with them on the search.

A torch, in case they had to look anywhere dark, Olivia thought. Under a shed or something like that. Smudge's favourite snacks. He really liked the little heart-shaped chicken ones. Olivia had done a taste test on five different sorts, and he always went for the chicken ones first. If he was stuck up a tree or anything like that, he would definitely come down for them.

What else? Olivia chewed the end of her pencil. A ladder? She wasn't sure Dad would want to carry one around.

"Oh, you're awake!" Mum put her head round Olivia's door. Olivia gazed up at her. Of course she was! How could she go back to sleep?

"Can I get up?" she asked eagerly.

Mum nodded. "Yes. But we're not going anywhere until you've had some breakfast. Just a quick bowl of cereal, that's all," she added, seeing Olivia was about to moan. "If you eat, you'll be able to hunt for him better."

Olivia dressed quickly, and then ran downstairs to gulp down the bowl of cereal that Mum insisted on. Then she fetched the torch and the snacks, and stood by the front door, waiting impatiently for Mum and Dad and Ben.

"What about Lucie?" she asked Mum, who was putting on her coat.

"I've texted her mum. It's still only seven-thirty, Olivia, I didn't want to get her out of bed. But I've told her where we'll be; she can call my mobile if she and Lucie want to come."

Dad gave an enormous yawn. "Everyone ready?"

They met Rob's dad halfway down Rob's road, crouching down to look under a big wheelie bin.

"No luck yet then?" Mum asked.

He shook his head. "Not yet. But he can't have gone far. I'm really sorry about this. Rob feels terrible. He's looking further up the road with his mum."

So he should! Olivia thought. But being furious with Rob didn't really help.

She and Ben and Mum and Dad set off up the road, calling and peering over fences. Olivia kept shaking the treats, hoping to see a little grey kitten dash eagerly towards her, like he did at home.

Half an hour later, they were back outside Rob's house, and everyone looked rather hopeless. Especially Rob. It seemed as though he'd been crying, and Olivia almost felt sorry for him.

"Not a sign," Dad said, frowning. "And none of the people we asked had spotted him."

"Should we go further? The next street?" Rob's mum asked doubtfully.

"Oh, look!" Mum pointed down the road.

"What is it? Can you see him?" Olivia gasped.

"Sorry, Olivia. It's Lucie, down at the end of the road, with her mum."

Lucie came runninng up the road as soon as she spotted Olivia. "We'll find him," she promised, seeing her friend's miserable face and hugging her tightly.

"I'm sure we will," her mum agreed, as they reached the little crowd outside Rob's house. "There's lots of us looking now."

Everyone was still discussing where to look next.

"He couldn't still be in your garden, hidden away?" Olivia suggested.

"We looked. We really did," Rob mumbled.

But his mum nodded. "We did, but if Smudge was frightened, he might have hidden himself. Maybe if Ben and Olivia went and called him? It's worth a try, anyway." She led them down the side of the house and into the back garden, and went inside to make some tea for everyone.

"Smudge! Smudge!" Olivia shook the cat treats again and again, and Ben jingled Smudge's favourite ball.

Lucie walked around the garden searching under all the bushes. But Smudge didn't appear. The garden was so quiet and empty.

I don't think we're ever going to find him, Olivia thought, staring sadly at the house. She knew Smudge had been here just last night, but he hadn't left even the tiniest clue. "Is that your window?" she asked Rob, who was lurking on the patio. She could see football stickers on a window that looked desperately high up. Had Smudge really climbed out of there?

Lucie gulped. "That's so high!"

Rob nodded miserably. "I think he must have jumped into that tree."

The girls went over to look at it. It was a plum tree – they could see the odd fruit still left at the top of the branches. It filled the gap between the house and the fence, and some of the branches spilled over the other side.

"What's over there?" Ben asked, trying to scramble up and grab the top of the fence.

"Just some old garages and stuff. There's an alley that runs from the road behind ours," Rob said. "But the fence is really solid. He couldn't have got under it. He must have gone round the side of the house and out the front."

But Olivia stared at the tree and the fence, thoughtfully. "What if he didn't go under the fence? Couldn't he have gone *over* it?"

"Of course not, look how tall it is..." Ben trailed off. "Oh! From the tree!"

Olivia nodded. "How do we get round there?"

Rob lead them round the side of the house, and Ben popped his head through the back door to explain they were going to look in the alleyway.

"We'll just be five minutes," he said quickly, and they vanished into the alley before anyone had time to stop them.

"Why didn't we think of it before?" Rob muttered, as they hurried off. "We just thought he must have gone out the front way."

The alley ran along halfway between Rob's house and the one next door, but they had to go into the next street to get into it. It was very narrow, with a row of tumbledown old garages – and lots of hiding places for a kitten.

"Smudge!" Olivia tore the treats packet open with her teeth, and shook out a handful.

Inside the garage, Smudge was pacing up and down by the hole in the wall. He had to keep trying – he had to get out! He scraped determinedly at the metal sheet, ignoring his sore paws. Then his ears pricked up suddenly as he heard the sound of a familiar voice. Was that Olivia? Had she come to find him? He scrabbled furiously at the wall again, trying to show her where he was.

"Hey, what was that?" Lucie said suddenly. "Something scratching!"

Everyone froze, holding their breath, waiting for the sound again.

"I can't hear anything!" Ben hissed.

"Shh! Listen, there it is again!" Lucie whispered.

Olivia jumped, dropping half the treats on the ground. "I heard it too! It must be him. Smudge, where are you?" she called.

There was silence for a minute, and then a loud, desperate meow.

"It is! It is! Where is he? Smudge, we're coming to find you!" Olivia called, running towards the garages.

Inside the garage, Smudge scrabbled at the metal again. He could hear Olivia! She'd come to find him. Furiously he scraped and scratched, mewing as loudly as he could. He had to make them hear him!

"Which one is it?" Ben asked.

"The one at the end, I think," Rob

said, smiling for the first time that morning. "He must be stuck somehow, he's trying to get out."

Olivia pushed her way past him, and crouched down by the garage wall. "He's here somewhere. Smudge… Smudge…"

A little grey paw suddenly stuck out from a hole in the concrete wall, where it had been patched together.

"He's there! I saw him. Oh, Smudge, we've missed you!" Olivia stroked the grubby little paw. "Look, his claws are all torn where he's been trying to get out." She sniffed, choking back sudden tears.

"How are we going to get him out?" Ben asked. "That hole isn't nearly big enough."

"What about this?" Rob held up a thick stick, which he'd found lying on the grass. "Couldn't we use it to pull that metal away a bit more?" He banged gently on the metal sheet, and the paw shot back inside as Smudge jumped back in fright.

"Don't scare him!" Olivia snapped.

Rob shook his head. "I had to, Olivia. If he was right behind the metal, I might hurt his paws with the stick."

"Oh." Olivia nodded.

Rob hooked the stick into the hole, and pulled. There was a creaking noise, and the thin metal bent a little.

"It's getting bigger! Here, I'll pull too." Ben added his weight to the stick, and Olivia knelt down by the hole.

"Don't be scared, Smudge, you'll be

out of there in a minute."

"There!" Ben said triumphantly. "That must be big enough. Good plan, Rob!"

Inside the garage, Smudge blinked at the hole, his whiskers quivering excitedly. He could hear Olivia. He edged forward, squeezing himself tightly against the concrete block, and suddenly tumbled forward out of the hole, and into Olivia's hands.

"Oh, Smudge, we've been looking everywhere." Olivia snuggled the kitten up against her chin, laughing and crying at the same time.

"Hey! You've found him!" Olivia's dad came running up the alley, with all the others hurrying behind him.

"He's fine," Olivia told them. "Just a bit dirty. He was stuck in that garage."

"We moved that bit of metal," Ben explained. "It was Rob who thought of it."

"But he wouldn't have run off and got stuck if I hadn't taken him first," Rob muttered. "I'll never do anything that stupid again, I promise."

"You're just lucky that you found him," his dad pointed out grimly.

"I know it was all my fault," Rob

muttered. "I said I'm really sorry, Dad."

"I think you'd better give some of your pocket money to the Rescue Centre by way of apology," his mum suggested, and Rob nodded.

Olivia looked over at Rob. "He only did it because he really wants a cat of his own," she murmured.

Rob's dad sighed. "Well, maybe when he proves he can be sensible enough to look after a kitten, he can have one. Which will take a long time!"

Olivia turned to Rob. "Rob, do you want to stroke Smudge too?"

Rob ran a gentle finger down the back of Smudge's head.

"Thanks," he whispered.

Now she had Smudge snuggled up and purring in her arms again, Olivia felt like she could forgive anything. Smudge pressed closer against her, looking nervously at Rob.

"It's OK, Smudge." She tickled him under the chin. "Rob's not going to hurt you." She smiled at Rob, only a small smile, but she got a huge one back.

Lucie reached out to rub Smudge's ears. "He's gorgeous. You're so lucky, Olivia!"

Olivia smiled. She was. Lucky to have Smudge – and even more lucky to have him back safe.

HOLLY WEBB

Holly Webb started out as a children's book editor, and wrote her first series for the publisher she worked for. She has been writing ever since, with over one hundred books to her name. Holly lives in Berkshire, with her husband and three young sons. Holly's pet cats are always nosying around when she is trying to type on her laptop.

For more information
about Holly Webb visit:

www.holly-webb.com